# Little Big Feet

Davidson 10/22/91 12.95

# Little

# Big Feet

by Ingrid and Dieter Schubert

Carolrhoda Books, Inc./Minneapolis

Somewhere between the sky and the earth is the land where witches live.

On this particular morning, all the witches were very upset. Little Irma was gone!

All the witches got on their broomsticks and flew around the land,
looking for Irma.

"Irma, where are you?" they shouted as they searched. "You've
really disappeared, haven't you? Please come back, Irma! We didn't
mean to laugh at you!"

But Irma did not answer. She had vanished.

That same morning, when Laura went to brush her teeth, she heard a soft snore. It was coming from under her drinking glass. Laura looked carefully and saw a tiny little witch lying there asleep!

"Hey," whispered Laura. "Hey you, wake up."

The witch jumped up. "Potzblitz! Who dares to wake me up?"

"I do," said Laura. "I would like to brush my teeth, if you don't mind. Say, are you a real witch?"

"Well, of course I am," Irma said huffily. Then she shuddered. "Brush your teeth? Pfui. That's not for me!"

She opened her mouth wide and showed Laura her teeth. "They're a beautiful shade of yellow, aren't they? I've never brushed them in my whole life!"

Laura reached for her toothbrush, but Irma grabbed it away from her.

"Hey," said the little witch, "That's my new broomstick. I think I'll fly away right now."

"Give me that!" shouted Laura. "Witches fly on broomsticks, not on toothbrushes. You must not be a real witch!"

"I am too a real witch!" cried Irma. And she got on the toothbrush and flew around the room. Then she took out a broken broomstick from under her coat.

"You see, I crashed this broomstick, and I need a new one. I want to go far away."

"Where?" Laura wanted to know.

"Anywhere, just far away," Irma sighed.

"Why?" asked Laura.

Irma landed on Laura's knee and said softly, "Just look at my feet. Do you notice anything?"

"No," said Laura. "I see plain feet. Big witch's feet."

"Yes!" Irma cried. "Big witch's feet! The other witches always laugh at me. 'Little Big Feet,' they call me. 'Irma has such big feet!' And I can't cast spells properly anymore either. I've forgotten the magic words. Every time I start to cast a spell, there's a great jolt all of a sudden — and my feet get bigger."

"You're making that up!" exclaimed Laura.

"I am not!" shouted Irma. "Okay, I'll cast a spell on you, since you don't believe me!"

She yelled a long, long word that sounded something like "kraxpoxboderhax," and suddenly her feet grew even bigger.

"Oh, no," she sobbed. "You see! I've forgotten the spell again, so my feet have gotten bigger. I think I must be getting old—even though I'm only 717. I'm afraid I'll never do any more magic!"

Laura tried to console Irma.

"Look at me," she said softly. "I have such big ears. The other children are always making fun of me. 'Laura Sail Ears,' they call me. 'Why don't you fly away, Laura!' But I can't fly, of course." Laura smiled. "Anyway—I like your big witch's feet."

"I like them too, actually," said Irma. "Only they look so plain and clunky."

"I know what we can do about that," said Laura. And she took out her paint set and brushes and sat down to work.

When she was finished, Irma shouted with joy, "I'm so happy! Now I have the most beautiful, happiest feet in the world! As a reward, I'll grant you whatever you wish."

But Laura didn't know what to wish for. And Irma didn't want to try casting any more spells.

"Let me brush my teeth first," said Laura. "I'm sure I'll think of something then."

Irma watched anxiously as Laura brushed her teeth.

"Does that hurt?" she asked.

"No, it just tickles a little bit. Do you want to try it?" asked Laura, offering the toothbrush to Irma.

At first Irma looked doubtfully at the toothbrush.
Then she tried it. After a minute, her teeth turned violet!
And then she cried, "The magic words! I remember them! The magic words have come back to me!"

"I can practice witchcraft again!" Irma yelled with a grin. "What shall I turn you into?"

Laura thought for a minute. "Make me into a dragon, but just a small one."

Irma mumbled and muttered and murmured. But it didn't work very well. Laura started to look a little bit like a dragon here and there, but then quickly changed back into a girl.

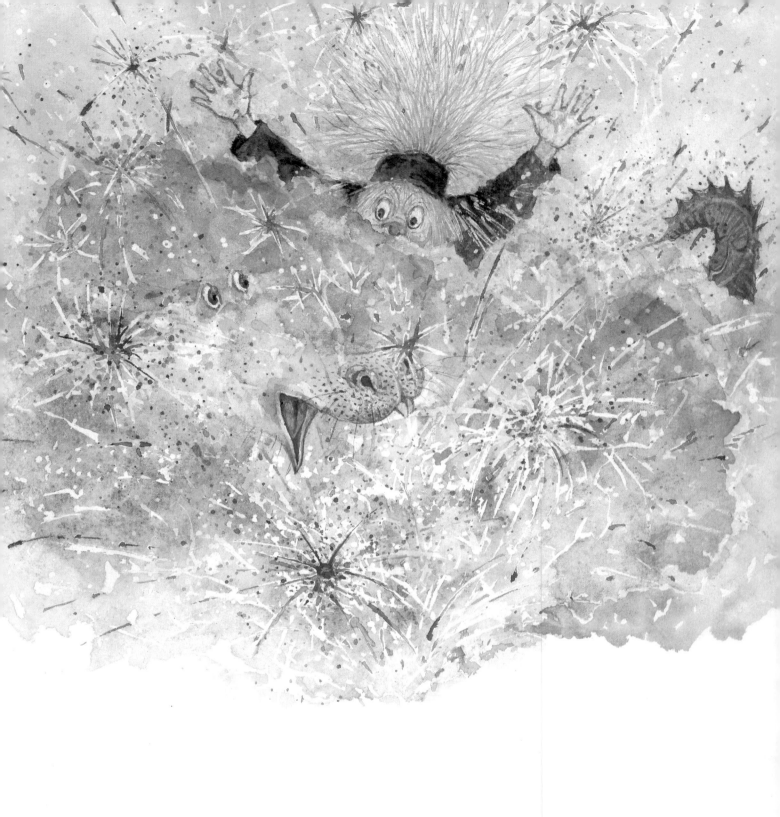

Suddenly there was a great deal of smoke and a strange hissing sound.
"Otto!" Irma shouted with delight.

"Irma! Here you are!" said Otto the dragon. "We all miss you so much. Since you've been away, we've had no one to make us laugh. Come on, we'll fly back together."

"Sure," said Irma. "But look at my feet first."

"Wow!" said Otto. "Those are the happiest witch's feet I've ever seen.
The others will be amazed. And what's happened to your teeth?"
"I'll explain that later," said Irma.

Laura was sad that Irma wanted to fly away with Otto. "Don't worry, Laura," said Irma. "We're sure to see each other again." Then she gave Laura a kiss on the left ear and a kiss on the right ear. "There's a present from me," she said. "Just wiggle your ears and you'll find out what it is."

With that, Irma and Otto flew away.

Laura wiggled her ears. And what do you suppose happened?
She began to sail through the air! She could fly! Now she could
really fly with her ears!

After a quick flight around the house, Laura landed beside her mother.

"Laura," gasped Mother, "who taught you how to do that?"

"Irma, the little witch," giggled Laura.

"You sure have some funny friends," said Mother.

Laura practiced flying the whole day long, and by the evening she could even perform tricks in the air. Father and Mother watched her, amazed.

Suddenly they were interrupted by a knock at the window.

An owl sat outside. He was carrying a letter in his beak.
"For Laura from Irma," croaked the owl. "I'll wait for your reply."

"You don't mean to tell me that now you can read, too," said
Laura's father.
"Well, of course I can," said Laura.

*And what do you think Laura replied to the little witch?*

Library of Congress Cataloging-in-Publication Data

Schubert, Ingrid, 1953-
    [Platvoetje. English]
    Little Big Feet / by Ingrid and Dieter Schubert ; [translated from
the Dutch by Amy Gelman].
        p.   cm.
    Translation of: Platvoetje.
    Summary: Laura, who has been teased about her big ears, is
sympathetic when she meets a tiny little witch with big feet.
ISBN 0-87614-426-1 (lib. bdg.) :
    [1. Individuality—Fiction. 2. Witches—Fiction.] I. Schubert,
Dieter, 1947-      . II. Title.
PZ7.S3834Li   1990
[E]—dc20                                              89-25279
                                                        CIP
                                                         AC

Manufactured in the United States of America

1  2  3  4  5  6  7  8  9  10  20  99  98  97  96  95  94  93  92  91  90